HOW TO MAKE A ROCK HAPPY

Illustrated by
Rachel Shead

A Guide to Laughing Wellness

By Tim Barlow

Melody loved watching clouds on a clear summer's day. They took on shapes that made her feel happy—rabbits, ducks, smiling faces, hearts and more. As she lay in the grass, looking up to the sky, she thought to herself…

"Grown-ups can be quite puzzling, and they don't always seem as happy as kids. My Grandad once told me that he's as strong as a rock, but there are few things that bring him joy. He said there aren't many reasons to be happy these days."

Melody thought about how rocks never seemed happy, just like her Grandad. This made her think a lot. Why were rocks different? What would make them happy? She felt curious and decided to go on an adventure to find out.

She remembered that her mom, dad, and teachers taught her that when she does things with a happy and hopeful heart, and when she helps others, she not only feels good about herself but also brings happiness to the people around her.

"You know what?" **Melody** said. "I'm determined to prove my Grandad wrong. I am going to find a way to make a grumpy old rock happy!"

Do you see anything in the picture that brings a smile to your face or makes you feel happy?

Melody was determined to make the rock happy and thought that music could be the key. She tried playing fast and then slow, using different instruments like the piano, drums, and recorder. However, no matter what melodies she created, the rock's mood didn't change.

She went to her mom and excitedly told her about her plan to make the rock happy. Her mom gently said, "Honey, rocks don't have feelings."

Melody felt surprised by her mom's words. She thought about her Grandad, who was as strong and solid as a rock. If rocks didn't have feelings, it meant her Grandad didn't either and she didn't want to believe that. **Melody** was determined to prove that the rock could be happy too. She wouldn't give up. She was going to find a way to make the rock happy, no matter what.

Let's spread some happiness through music!
Use the keyboard below to play a cheerful tune that fills your heart with joy and puts a big smile on your face!

Melody has a special talent for bringing happiness to her friends when they are feeling sad. She tells them funny jokes that act like magic spells, making them laugh and feel full of joy once more. **Melody** wondered if her jokes could make the rock laugh too.

"What do you get when you cross a rock and a roll?" she asked the rock excitedly. "Rock and roll music!"

No response.

"Why did the rock go to school? To get a little boulder!"

Not even a wink.

"What's a rock's favorite type of music? Heavy rock!"

The rock remained unmoved and didn't make a peep.

No matter how hard she tried or how many jokes she told, the rock just didn't seem to understand or respond to any of them.

Share your funniest jokes with everyone! Use the microphone below to tell your best jokes and bring a little bit of joy into everyone's life!

Melody had a bright idea! She thought the rock might have fun bouncing with her on a trampoline. Trampolines were very exciting, and she wanted to share that joy with the rock.

With a big leap, **Melody** jumped onto the trampoline, urging the rock to bounce together. But as the rock hopped up and down, something seemed wrong. The rock didn't show any signs that it was having fun.

Undeterred, **Melody** tried different jumps and flips, hoping to spark some excitement in the rock. But no matter how high she jumped or how fancy her tricks were, the rock seemed even more uncomfortable. It didn't find the bouncing as enjoyable as she did.

Then, something unexpected happened! The rock bounced off the trampoline by mistake and landed in a nearby bush. **Melody** hurried over to save it, gently picking it up and making sure it was okay. She felt worried. It seemed like the trampoline adventure didn't make the rock any happier.

Get ready to bounce to happiness! Use the finger trampoline below to show us all the cool tricks that make you feel like you are jumping with joy!

Melody tried everything she could think of to make the rock happy. She juggled with rolled up socks, hoping the rock would laugh at her silly tricks. She played sports and invited the rock to join in. **Melody** even baked yummy cupcakes, imagining the rock enjoying their tasty flavors. To entertain the rock, she turned on the TV, hoping the colourful shows would make it smile. She drew pretty pictures, but they didn't seem to catch the rock's attention. **Melody** didn't mind getting messy, so she happily jumped in muddy puddles, encouraging the rock to join in the playful splashing. After all the fun, she snuggled up with her cat, hoping the warmth and coziness would bring happiness to the rock.

But no matter what **Melody** did, the rock stayed quiet and motionless, showing no signs of happiness. This made her feel a little sad, leaving her wondering what the rock needed to find its inner joy.

Do you have any other fun activities that you enjoy doing? Maybe Melody could try them to make the rock happy!

Melody felt sad and disappointed. She thought to herself, "Do rocks always stay dull and grey? That seems so boring and unhappy." Then, she looked at herself in the mirror and wondered, "Why can't I make the rock feel happy?"

When **Melody** saw that she was making a sad face, she decided to change it. She slowly turned her frown into a big, bright smile. Then, she made the silliest and funniest face that she could think of! It was so silly that she couldn't help but burst into laughter!

Once she calmed down, **Melody** had a fun idea and started exploring how different faces could change the way she felt. First, she accidentally made herself laugh while looking puzzled, scrunching her eyebrows, and tilting her head. Then, she made a surprised face with wide eyes and raised eyebrows, which made her giggle. She then pretended to be shocked as she placed her hands on her cheeks. Can you believe it? She even started laughing while pretending to cry! Finally, she made the happiest face she could imagine, with wide-open eyes and a wonderful smile that lit up the whole room!

Try pulling a face with your eyes wide open, wiggling your ears and sticking your bottom lip out. Let your imagination run wild and see how making different faces makes you feel!

Filled with excitement, **Melody** had another brilliant idea. She took a paintbrush and her colourful paint set and started painting the rock. With just a few careful brush strokes, a big, funny smile appeared on the rock, and to her amazement, she could imagine the rock laughing out loud! To make it even more joyful, she added big, goofy eyes and spikey hair which made the rock look even happier than before!

Can you describe how you would paint the rock to make it look even sillier or funnier? Can you think of some fun and wacky ways to make the rock look even more joyful?

Melody was so overjoyed by how lively and cheerful her new painted rock looked that she couldn't wait to paint more rocks right away! As she painted more faces on different rocks, something amazing happened. Each rock had its own special personality, and they seemed to come alive!

Melody gave some rocks big, wide smiles that stretched from ear to ear. Others had cheeky grins or sweet, happy smiles that made her heart melt. She added big, round eyes to some rocks, while others had tiny, twinkling eyes that made them seem very playful. And the noses! Some rocks had little button noses, while others had long, pointy noses that made them look really funny!

Every rock was unique and special in its own way. They came in different sizes, shapes, and colours. Some rocks were big and tough, like they could handle anything! And there were some rocks that were just so adorable and tiny, you couldn't help but smile at them. **Melody** even found some special rocks that sparkled in the sunshine, as if they had secret magical powers!

As **Melody** gathered her painted rock friends together, they looked like a happy family. Each rock had its own special appearance that made it unique, and this brought a heartwarming smile to her face.

Do you have a favorite rock that Melody painted? Which one do you like the most and why?

Melody gathered her collection of painted rocks and headed to the park near her school. With great care, she arranged them in a special way, just like students sitting in a classroom. She cleared her throat and then spoke loudly, "Today, we are going to have a fantastic time learning about the many ways people laugh. When we laugh together, something magical happens. It brings us closer to one another, helps us create special connections, and those connections can fill our hearts with happiness."

"Ha, ha, ha!" is the most common laughing sound that we make when something is highly amusing or funny. It shows that we are having a good time and brings joy to everyone around us. Let's try laughing together using the "ha" sound!

"Ho, ho, ho!" is the deep and jolly sound that Santa Claus makes as he spreads joy around the world. It can be heard from far away, filling everyone's hearts with happiness. Why don't we all try laughing as we make the "ho" sound!

"He, he, he!" is a silly little giggle when we can't contain our excitement and when we want to share wonderful news with our friends. It's a sound that bubbles up from deep inside and fills us with pure joy! Let's all giggle together with the "he" sound!

"Hi, hi, hi!" is a cheerful, high-pitched laughter sound that bursts out when we share a funny joke or have an amazing time with friends. It's a sound that lifts our spirits and fills the air with happiness. Let's all join in and laugh making the "hi" sound together!

Take a deep breath and get ready to laugh with the Ha, Ho, He, and Hi sounds. As you let out each sound, pay attention to how it makes you feel. Does the 'Ha' sound make your belly shake with laughter? Does the 'Ho' sound feel like it's coming from deep within your belly? Does the 'He' sound give you a playful tingle in your throat? And what about the 'Hi' sound? Is it a high-pitched sound and does it make your whole face light up with joy?

Melody's friend, Harmony, who was playing on the school play structure, heard Melody's laughter and became curious. With a friendly smile, Harmony asked, "Melody, what's making you laugh so much?" **Melody** explained that she was trying to make rocks happy by painting silly faces on them and teaching them how to laugh.

Excitedly, Harmony responded, "That sounds like a lot of fun! Can I join in? I have some other ideas we can try that might make them laugh."

Together, they tried different ways of laughing to find out which one made them the happiest!

They laughed fast, slow, quietly, loudly, lying down, while jumping around, with their tongues out and then with their lips closed. They even pretended to make the laughing sounds that they thought different animals would make.

The more they laughed, the louder and more energetic they became. They had so much fun that they ended up rolling around on the floor, laughing together in pure joy!

Can you think of any other ways of laughing? You could try laughing softly, loudly, with a snort, or even with a funny hiccup. Let your imagination run wild and discover new ways to spread laughter and happiness!

As the sun started to set, **Melody** rushed back to her Grandad's house, full of excitement. Grasped tightly in her hand was a beautifully painted rock, decorated with a super funny and colorful face that made her giggle. She couldn't wait to share her discovery with her Grandad.

"Grandad," she said with a big smile, "You were right when you said rocks can't be happy. But guess what? I found happiness in fun activities, drawing silly faces on rocks, and laughing with my friends!"

Grandad smiled back at her, happy to see her so joyful. "You've learned something important, **Melody**," he said. "Even though I'm not happy all the time, spending time with the people I love brings me the most happiness!" Then, he playfully asked, "Why don't we grab some paintbrushes and make Grandad and Granddaughter rocks? It will be fun to create something special together!"

So, off they went, painting, laughing, and making beautiful memories that would forever bring smiles to their faces.

Tim Barlow (The Laughing Lion) is a British/Canadian musician, songwriter, and father of two. He actively promotes Laughter Wellness to enrich the Canadian Prairies and send peace, love, and joy out into the universe. In his music career, he has over twenty years of on-stage experience across Europe and Canada, and after starting a family, he gravitated towards writing and performing children's music. Described as the English Fred Penner, he juggles stories of family life with laughter and movement songs to engage his audience in a campfire sing-along experience. His life mission is to promote love, good health, and happiness through Laughter Wellness, music, and the performing arts.

◆ FriesenPress

One Printers Way
Altona, MB R0G 0B0
Canada

www.friesenpress.com

Illustrator: Rachel Shead

ISBN
978-1-03-919144-0 (Hardcover)
978-1-03-919143-3 (Paperback)
978-1-03-919145-7 (eBook)

1. JUVENILE FICTION, FAMILY

Distributed to the trade by The Ingram Book Company

Milton Keynes UK
Ingram Content Group UK Ltd.
UKHW050248280524
443283UK00002B/2

9 781039 191433